£3.95

MASTERS OF THE UNIVERSE™

ANNUAL 1989

CONTENTS

World

Copyright © MCMLXXXVIII by Mattel Inc.
All rights reserved throughout the world.
Published in Great Britain by
World International Publishing Limited,
An Egmont Company,
Egmont House, P.O. Box 111, Great Ducie Street,
Manchester M60 3BL.
Printed in Italy.
ISBN 7235 6834 0

BAT ATTACK

PART ONE

As he sat at the heavy oak table located in the cavernous banqueting hall of Eternos Palace, Fisto felt decidedly out of place. He was facing two important visitors and, despite his best attempts at small talk, they seemed uninterested in him and his opinions. From further along the banqueting table he could hear the animated chatter of Man-At-Arms, Teela and the other Heroic Warriors. They were enjoying themselves. Everyone was enjoying themselves.

Everyone except Fisto.

He leaned backwards and yawned. His flimsy wooden chair groaned in protest as he shifted his great weight. This wasn't the type of party he'd expected. This was a formal banquet, and Fisto hated formal banquets!

Not that he could have chosen to stay away. The banquet had been organized as part of the celebrations for Queen Marlena's birthday and Fisto had been ordered to attend by Royal decree. At first he had been looking forward to the gathering. It wasn't often that all the Heroic Warriors were collected in one place, and Fisto had been eager to renew acquaintances with the likes of Roboto and Mekaneck. He was also pleased to have been given the opportunity to meet many of the new heroes like Rio Blast and Snout Spout.

However, his hopes that the event would be an informal affair were dashed when he learned that dukes, duchesses and important people from all over Eternia were planning to attend. And, as if to add insult to injury, Prince Adam had casually told him that each of the guests was to present Queen Marlena with a special gift. Apparently this was a custom on Marlena's home world, Earth, where such gifts were known as birthday presents. The queen had received many wondrous novelties and trinkets.

Stratos, the Avion leader, had brought with him a mottled egg. It was as large as a man's hand and its shell was decorated with exotic flame-coloured jewels that seemed to dance and

sparkle with a life of their own. Buzz-Off had brought a small container of golden honey collected, at great personal risk, from the hives of Eternia's giant bees.

Fisto had brought an axe.

For weeks before the banquet he had been unable to think of a suitable present, and then he'd remembered an old saying of his father's: "You always know where you are with an axe!" And the axe Fisto had given the queen was the sharpest, most expertly balanced throwing axe on all Eternia.

Fisto had been quite proud of his choice of present and, if truth be told, he still was, despite the strange glance he received from the queen

quivering in its ornate serving bowl, Fisto couldn't imagine why. He could barely stand to look at it, let alone eat it! No, he was a man of simple tastes, and he was perfectly satisfied with a crust of bread and a hunk of cheese.

Fisto sighed wearily. The banquet hadn't turned into the rousing party he'd expected and he couldn't wait for it to come to an end. Restlessly, he turned in his chair and stared vacantly out of an arch-shaped window.

Outside, in the distance, he could see an orchard of fruit trees. They were covered in a thick blanket of pink blossom, and they were swaying gently in the light breeze. The sun was high in the sky. It was a typically peaceful summer's afternoon.

Suddenly, something dark and shadowy appeared in the sky. Fisto watched it growing larger, coming closer. But it wasn't a shadow at all – it was an unruly mass of winged figures! Their eyes were shining a fiery red and they were flying directly towards the palace. They were going to – *KERRASH!* In a shower of splintered glass, the winged figures smashed through the window, knocking Fisto and many of the other guests to the floor.

Stunned by the unexpected attack, Fisto slowly picked himself up. The banqueting hall had erupted into chaos. People were running this way and that, and the flying creatures were swooping down on them. Dozens more of the creatures were perched on top of the table. They were over two metres tall and, although they were humanoid in appearance, they bore a striking resemblance to bats. Their faces were thin, with large wolfish eyes. They were covered in short grey hair, more like a patchy fuzz than real fur, and their coarse leathery wings were now folded tightly against their backs. Seemingly mindless, they were eating everything that they could lay their hands on...food, cutlery, even pieces of glass. It was all scooped up in their taloned hands and crushed between their powerful jaws.

Fisto could see Rio Blast standing in front of a distraught Queen Marlena, shielding her with his body. His teeth were tightly clenched, and he was using his blasters to fire a constant barrage of missiles and laser beams at an ever-advancing group of bat-creatures. The blasts were striking home, but were merely bouncing off the creatures' surprisingly tough hides. Suddenly, the bat-creatures let loose ear-splitting shrieks. They surged forward and engulfed Rio.

when he presented her with the axe. But, apart from his inspired choice of present, Fisto wasn't enjoying the banquet. For a start there was hardly anything to eat... anything tasty, at least.

The table was loaded with all manner of strange-looking dishes and, as yet, Fisto hadn't summoned up the courage to taste any of them. There was a soup decorated with a blue, shimmering garnish and despite assurances to the contrary, Fisto was convinced that this was glowing moss collected from the Mountains of Mourne. There were brightly coloured casseroles and blue-black cheeses, but it was the Eternian squid that really turned Fisto's stomach. It was supposedly a rare delicacy, but as he watched it

Fisto had seen enough! Shaking off his grogginess, he leapt over the banqueting table and ploughed into the group of bat-creatures surrounding the queen. His mighty steel-gloved fist struck once, twice...three times. One after another, the bat-creatures fell to the floor. Brute strength was succeeding where laser beams and blasters had failed. Fisto was grinning wildly – he was in his element, battling against the forces of evil. "Don't worry, my lady," he said to the queen confidently, "I'll soon have..."

Fisto's words trailed off as one of the bat-creatures suddenly swooped down upon him. He dropped, stunned, to the ground.

The bat-creatures regrouped and, with a chorus of inhuman laughter and a flurry of leathery wings, they shambled closer to Queen Marlena. Matching them step for step, the queen slowly backed away. She knew she could not hold out against the monsters alone. But she wasn't alone! Although his pace was slow and ponderous, Prince Adam was running towards her. For some unfathomable reason he was reaching behind his back as if about to draw an invisible sword from an equally invisible scabbard...

With a deep growl, a bat-creature broke off from the main pack, turned, and lurched towards the prince. The queen cried out, trying to warn her son of the danger, but the words froze in her throat as the creature grasped Prince Adam and hoisted him high into the air. With a casual shrug of its powerful shoulders it tossed the bewildered prince out of the shattered window.

Like a discarded rag doll, Adam struck the soft earth outside. Gasping for breath, he climbed to his feet. What had he been thinking of! In his confusion and haste to save his mother, he had nearly revealed his secret identity! Still, he was grateful to the bat-creature for throwing him outside. At least here he was free from prying eyes. He drew his magic sword and proudly held it aloft. "By the Power of Grayskull!" he exclaimed. "I have the Power!"

The mystical power of the Eternian Elders surged through the sword and enveloped him in a

field of crackling energy. His whole body seemed to grow and expand and then, with a thunderous roar and a fiery explosion Adam, Prince of Eternia, was transformed into He-Man, the mightiest man in the universe.

He-Man vaulted through the window back into the banqueting hall. He landed in a crouched position, looking from side to side. He quickly assessed the situation. His mother was now backed against a cold stone wall and the bat-creatures were standing in a loose circle around her. His anger growing with each passing second, He-Man raised his power sword and fired a silver-blue blast of electricity at the milling band of winged monsters. The shimmering energy blast struck one of the bat-creatures. It staggered and fell.

"GROWWRR!" The main pack howled in unison as if they shared their fallen companion's anguish, and with a furious beating of their powerful wings, they took to the air, launching themselves at He-Man.

Taken by surprise, the mighty Eternian hero was bowled over. The bat-creatures piled on top of him. More of the creatures left the banqueting table, where they had been gorging themselves,

and joined in the battle. He-Man struck out with his power sword, knocking one of them away, but four more took its place. It was hopeless! He-Man's head began to spin, his vision to blurr...

"Ha, ha, ha!" Skeletor's hideous cackle echoed throughout the dank caves, located deep inside Snake Mountain. He was bent low over his magical cauldron, and in its foul, stagnant waters an image of the recent events at the Royal Palace of Eternos was slowly beginning to fade.

"I was right! The Heroic Warriors proved powerless against the bat-creatures. Powerless!" laughed the living skeleton. His long bony face twisted into an evil expression that more resembled anger than joy.

But joy was what he was feeling!

The bat-creatures had landed everywhere on Eternia and in their wake they'd left a trail of

mindless destruction. Field after field of vital crops had been consumed by the greedy monsters. Across the entire planet, all was chaos and confusion. Chaos wrought by Skeletor, for it had been he who had called the bat-creatures to Eternia!

With a cold, inhuman chuckle he turned and walked over to a vast monster of a machine. The contraption was all wires, an intricate network of glowing cables that connected a simple computer console to an enormous radar dish. The device was painted silver and gold, and contrasted sharply with the green, moss-covered walls of the cave. The radar dish was slowly rotating, continuously transmitting a sequence of high-pitched notes into space. It had been doing this for many days. It was the beacon that had attracted the winged monsters to Eternia.

The bat-creatures were deep-space inhabitants. They migrated from one part of the galaxy to another, to any planet that lay in their path. The creatures would land on such worlds and devour anything that they could find. Once they had eaten their fill they would continue their travels, mindless of the destruction left behind them. They navigated by sonic waves, and it had been a simple matter for Skeletor to create his machine and use it to emit sounds of a particular frequency and bring the bat-creatures to Randor's wretched world.

When the winged monsters had entered Eternia's atmosphere, Skeletor and his evil followers had secured themselves deep within Snake Mountain where they would be safe from harm. Soon, Skeletor would switch off his machine, the bat-creatures would leave, the Heroic Warriors would be defeated, and Skeletor would emerge from his hiding place to find a devastated world. A world powerless to prevent his conquest! The Master of Evil threw back his head and laughed manically. He had done it. After years of battle, after years of defeat, he had finally done it!

"I heard you laughing, Lord Skeletor," Evil-Lyn said, entering the cave. "Do you find something amusing?"

"Oh yes!" Skeletor gloated. "I find something extremely amusing. You see, I've won. At last, I've won!"

Has Skeletor really won? What has happened to He-Man and the Heroic Warriors? Turn to page 28 for the second chapter of Bat Attack.

11

MASTER mind!

Spot the Differences

At first glance, the two pictures below appear to be identical. There are, however, six minor differences. Can you spot them? Check your answers at the bottom of the page.

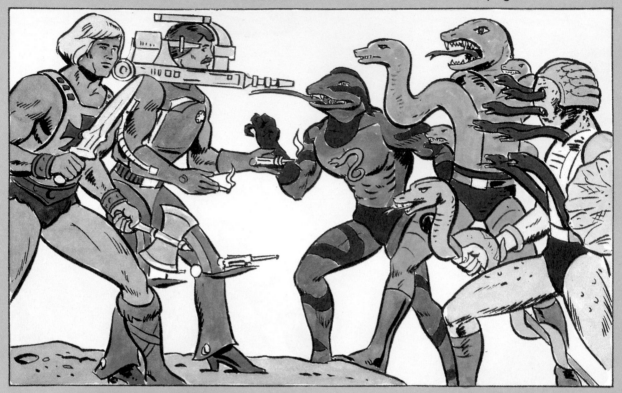

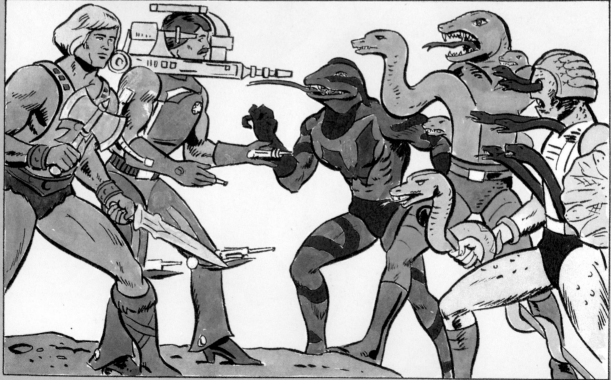

Answers

12

SNOUT SPOUT

NAME: SNOUT SPOUT

HEIGHT: 1·78 metres

WEIGHT: 102 kilograms

EYES: Robotic

HAIR: None

GROUP AFFILIATION: The Heroic Warriors

CHARACTER PROFILE: Snout Spout was a handsome Etherian peasant who was captured by Hordak and transformed into a half-man, half-robotic cyborg. Using alien methods of mind control, Hordak broke Snout Spout's will and forced him to join the Evil Horde. However, when the Horde crossed over to Eternia, Snout Spout was able to throw off Hordak's influence, and he defected to the Heroic Warriors.

He is able to use his trunk to fire powerful water blasts, and his cyborg nature gives him partial super-strength. Despite these amazing attributes, Snout Spout lacks confidence in himself. He fails to see the vital contribution he makes in the fight against evil. This lack of self-esteem is compounded by the embarrassment he feels over his appearance. He refuses to look at his reflection in a mirror and often thinks that his fellow Heroic Warriors are laughing at him behind his back.

He-Man and Man-At-Arms have promised to help change Snout Spout back to his human form, but so far they've met with nothing but failure.

Snout Spout's best friend is Orko, and the diminutive Sorcerer has helped train him in the art of fire-fighting.

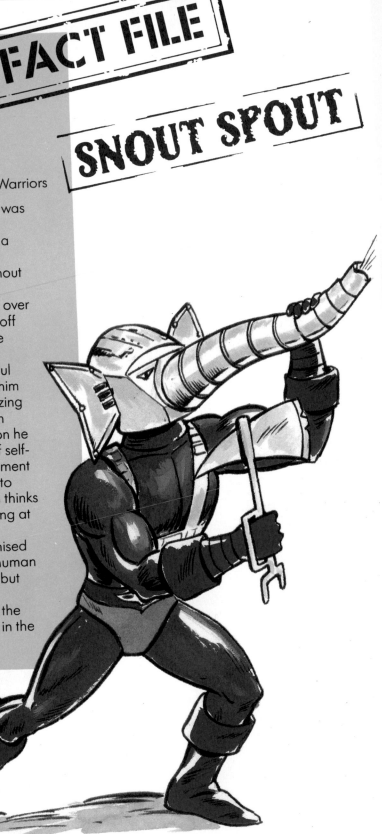

15

NAME: RIO BLAST

HEIGHT: 1·73 metres

WEIGHT: 69 kilograms

EYES: Brown

HAIR: Brown

GROUP AFFILIATION: The Heroic Warriors

CHARACTER PROFILE: Although shorter than many of his fellow Heroic Warriors, Rio Blast still packs quite a punch. At first glance he appears normal, but at the slightest mental command he is able to transform himself into a walking arsenal as lasers miraculously sprout from hidden cavities in his chest and wrists. Blasters spring from his knees and, with a simple flick of his head, he can command the awesome power of a photon cannon.

For many years, Rio was the 'law' in the Lost Starband, where he valiantly fought against injustice. However, before he was able to completely tame that wild frontier, he accidentally stumbled into a Space Warp, and found himself stranded on Eternia, where he joined with He-Man in the battle against Hordak and Skeletor. However, he wants to return home, and He-Man has promised to do all he can to help him do just that.

As well as being the fastest draw in the universe, Rio is a skilled mechanic and he often repairs and modifies his own weapons systems. He has a short temper and, although this sometimes causes friction with the other heroes, he is always the first to apologize.

GRAYSKULL BESIEGED

Darill was sitting on the bank of a steep hill. From his vantage point he could clearly see the twenty or so wicker huts that made up his small village. They were positioned next to each other in an almost haphazard fashion, and they were encircled by a tall, wooden fence. Outside the squat buildings Darill could see children running this way and that, playing with gaudily painted balls and crude hoops made from strips of tree bark. How they summoned up the energy for such activity on this hot summer's afternoon, Darill had no idea.

Standing beside the children were the village women. They were chatting, casually keeping a watchful eye on their sons and daughters. And, although he was too far away to see them, Darill guessed that a number of recently modelled clay pots had been placed outside the huts to dry in the sun.

With a smile Darill lay back on the grass. Village life was good but he could hardly wait for the following summer when he would leave his home and travel to the Royal Palace of Eternos.

Every year, each Eternian village selected its brightest, most capable boy to become a page boy to King Randor. This year Darill had been chosen by his village, and when he turned ten he would be able to take up his duties. He would be taught the arts of chivalry and knighthood, he would learn how to live off the land, how to defend himself, and how to ride beautiful white-maned stallions.

Still, all that was nearly a year away and there was more than enough to occupy Darill's time until then. His father often needed help hunting game, and there were always chores to be done at home. And then there were the statues.

There were three statues in all, located in a field to the west of Darill's village. Carved from enormous boulders, they resembled giant stone heads and they were easily four times as tall as Darill. Rumour had it that they dated from the time of the Eternian Elders, and over the centuries the elements had scarred and blistered their blue-grey faces. Rain and hail had relentlessly pounded them, giving their once smooth surfaces a rough, pitted texture. The wind had caused great cracks to appear in the statues and one seemed to have a hideous scar stretching diagonally across its left eye. Great wads of moss had grown on the stone faces, and at night this seemed to glow an eerie green. In fact, it was said that evil spirits lurked within the statues. However, they seemed harmless enough, and Darill and his friends spent many hours playing on or around them.

But not today. Today, Darill was content to lie back on the grass, close his eyes and dream.

Dream of palaces and knights, and of beautiful white-maned stallions.

Darill drifted into a light sleep, but was soon awakened by an ear-splitting roar. The hill was vibrating and trees were crashing violently to the ground. Darill slammed his eyes shut and fiercely dug his fingers into the grassy bank. What was happening? What?!

Darill's question was answered when he looked over at the field behind the village. He could see the three statues...and they were moving! At first the giant heads merely swayed back and forth. Then, without warning, three pairs of colossal arms burst from beneath the ground. Hoisting themselves up on these arms, the statues pulled free of the earth, revealing bodies that had lain hidden for centuries. Like the heads, the bodies were grey and craggy.

As the statues rose to their full height, the shockwaves caused by their sudden awakening began to die down. The creatures towered above

the surrounding landscape and Darill's parents, along with the other villagers, ran from their homes in an effort to escape them. However, the statues seemed uninterested in the fleeing people and, as if on cue, they each flexed their mighty muscles.

Darill gasped. He had thought that the statues were made entirely of stone, but he was wrong. As the creatures moved, the stone cracked and fell away. Beneath it lay gleaming metal. The statues weren't statues at all – they were giant androids! They were coloured silver, and their sleek, slender bodies were dotted with flashing, coloured lights. Their eyes were deeply sunken and glowed an emerald green.

The androids turned as one and slowly marched away, casually striding over the fearful villagers as they moved past the wicker huts. Then the sound of sinister laughter filled the air. It was easily recognizable as Hordak's high-pitched cackle. Darill looked upwards and high above him he could just make out the shape of a Horde fighter craft.

Hordak was obviously responsible for activating the androids, and Darill guessed that he was now directing them towards Castle Grayskull. But legends told of how, if Grayskull fell, evil would sweep the land. Darill knew he couldn't let that happen. He knew he had to find He-Man and put a stop to Hordak's evil plan. A determined expression on his face, he leapt to his feet and began to run in the direction of the Royal Palace of Eternos.

Inside the Horde fighter craft, Hordak turned to his evil follower, Grizzlor. "It has worked!" he cried, pointing at a small black box. "The re-energizer I invented has awakened the androids!"

"Huh," Grizzlor muttered to himself, "I still don't understand why we haven't used the androids to attack Grayskull before now."

"I heard that, you fool!" shouted Hordak. "How could we have used the androids? Until now, we assumed they were stone statues!"

"We did?" Grizzlor asked dimly.

"Of course!" Hordak replied, growing increasingly angry with his dim lieutenant. "However, while subduing the Outer Planets, Horde Prime learned that the statues were really warrior robots. Apparently, hundreds of years ago they conquered half the galaxy, but when they tried to invade Eternia, they were defeated and imprisoned in stone by the Elders. Over the years everyone forgot about the androids and took them to be mere stone statues."

"Oh, now I remember!" Grizzlor exclaimed, a strange gleam in his eye. "Horde Prime ordered us to reactivate the androids and then send them to him. He hopes to use them in his future conquests!"

"Well...er...yes!" Hordak replied, more than a little surprised at Grizzlor's sensible words. "But before we dispatch them to the Outer Planets we're going to use them in a little conquest of our own." And with this he piloted the fighter craft back to the Fright Zone, content in the knowledge that the radio waves being emitted by his re-energizer box would compel the androids to lay siege to Castle Grayskull.

Safe behind the magical defences of Castle Grayskull, the Sorceress was unaware of the approaching danger. For days she had been lost in mystical study, yet now some uncanny sixth sense told her to leave her books and parchments. She climbed up to Grayskull's time-worn battlements. There, she suddenly froze in her tracks. Her eyes widened and her heart began to beat wildly, for the sight that greeted her was enough to strike fear even in her brave soul.

The three giant androids had appeared on the horizon, and ancient trees and young saplings alike were buckling beneath them as they loomed even closer.

"By the Elders!" cried the Sorceress, guessing the androids' grim intention. "I must prevent them from reaching the castle."

With this she transformed herself into Zoar, the fighting falcon of force! She spread her mighty wings and propelled herself from the battlements. As straight as an arrow, Zoar streaked towards the monstrous attackers. Then, as she drew closer to her targets, she plunged into an attack dive and launched two missiles from her back-mounted photon cannon.

The missiles landed on the ground directly in front of the androids. They detonated in a thunderous explosion, throwing debris and rubble high into the air, but when the dust finally settled, Zoar saw to her astonishment that the missiles had hardly slowed the androids. The great, ponderous creatures were still continuing towards Grayskull, which now lay only a few kilometres ahead of them.

Suddenly the arm of the lead android snaked upwards and Zoar was caught in its mighty fist. She was trapped! And the android was tightening its grip...

In a desperate bid for freedom, Zoar used her beak to break through the casing on the android's enormous hand. Beneath the casing there was a thick metal bar, similar in design to a human bone. Above this there was a confusing mass of criss-crossing wires and cables. Zoar guessed that this was the equivalent of a man's

nervous system and, with the aid of her magical talons, she ripped and tore at the brightly coloured wires. This caused the android to release its grip, and Zoar quickly flew free.

Mustering all her remaining strength, she flew back to Grayskull. Once inside she became the Sorceress and collapsed, exhausted, on the cold stone floor.

Outside, the androids had reached the castle and were now pounding on the force shield that surrounded it. Soon they would break through – and the Sorceress was powerless to stop them.

At the Royal Palace of Eternos, King Randor was discussing security matters with Teela, He-Man and Rio Blast. "Hmm, I think you're right, Teela," the king said, thoughtfully. "Hordak and Skeletor have been much too quiet of late. Perhaps we should double the palace guard, just in case they're up to their usual..."

Randor's words trailed off as Darill suddenly burst in through the heavy wooden doors of the throne room. The boy had crossed many kilometres of inhospitable territory and the lower parts of his legs were caked in mud.

"K-King Randor," he gasped, "H-Hordak's using the statues to attack Grayskull. But they're not statues, th-they're a-androids and if...and if..."

"Whoa there, boy!" Rio said. "Take it easy. Once you've gotten your breath back, you can tell us all about it."

Soon Darill had recovered sufficiently to describe all he had seen to the Heroic Warriors.

"What?" cried Teela. "I don't believe it!"

"Believe it," said He-Man calmly. "Nothing about Hordak surprises me. Come on, we've got to get over to Grayskull – fast!"

Minutes later the Heroic Warriors were outside in the courtyard. Rio Blast was climbing behind the controls of the Wind Raider, and close by He-Man and Teela were mounting two Jet Sleds.

The three flying craft suddenly soared high into the sky, the sound of their engines violently shattering the peace and tranquillity of the Royal Palace. For a split second the Heroic Warriors hovered above Eternos, as if mentally preparing themselves for the forthcoming conflict. Then, without a word passing between them, they piloted their craft in the direction of Castle Grayskull.

Night had begun to fall by the time the group finally reached their destination. In the darkness, the lights on the androids' bodies made them appear like ghostly giants. Seemingly tireless, they had surrounded Grayskull and were continuing in their efforts to breach the invisible force field that protected the ancient fortress.

"By Eternia's twin moons!" exclaimed Teela. "I had no idea the androids would be so huge!"

"Well, as an old rancher friend of mine used to say," Rio cried, piloting the Wind Raider down towards the androids, "the taller they are, the harder they fall!"

"No! Rio, come back!" He-Man shouted after his reckless friend, but his words fell on deaf ears and, after switching the Wind Raider to autopilot, Rio leapt from the craft.

"Geronimo!" the cosmic gunslinger yelled as he fell towards the ground.

Directly beneath him lay one of the androids and, as he neared it, Rio pulled down his head cannon, flipped out his knee blasters and switched his hand pistols to firing mode. With a laugh he launched a barrage of laser blasts and photon missiles at the giant machine. The blasts struck home, the android staggered backwards and then, as if nothing had happened, it resumed

its attack on Grayskull's defences.

Performing a complicated series of somersaults, Rio landed on the soft, sandy ground immediately in front of the android.

"Ignore me, will you?" he cried. "Well, let's see you laugh this off!"

A second burst of firepower struck the android dead centre. Again it seemed to have little effect. As the monstrous creature continued to pound on the invisible force field with its left fist, it raised its right hand and casually flicked Rio away. He flew backwards and struck his head on a large boulder.

"Rio!" Teela cried out, hastily steering her Jet Sled towards her fallen companion.

Her concern had blinded her to the obvious danger, and the android struck out a second time. Swatting the Jet Sled out of the sky, it sent the

craft crashing to the ground. Teela was thrown clear of the wreckage and she landed, stunned, on the soft earth.

A short distance away, ensuring that he remained beyond the reach of the androids, He-Man landed his own Jet Sled. If only Rio hadn't acted so rashly. But at least He-Man had seen the androids in combat, and he now thought he knew of a way to put them out of action...permanently!

Using his magical Power Sword, He-Man transmitted a mental message inside Castle Grayskull. "Sorceress, you must use your powers to make Grayskull invisible," he said.

"But to do that I will have to lower the defence shield," the Sorceress transmitted back, clearly weakened by her ordeal. "And, invisible or not, that would leave Grayskull open to the androids' attack!"

"Please, trust me."

"Very well," the Sorceress said and from within the confines of Grayskull, she weaved her magic. Slowly the ancient fortress became translucent, then completely invisible.

The androids stopped suddenly and glowered at one another, confused expressions on their faces. Then, as if enormous pressures were building up within their bodies, steam began seeping from their joints. The metallic monsters staggered and fell to the ground, throwing up great billowing clouds of dirt. Floundering in the sand, the androids tried to pick themselves up. The steam was continuing to seep from their bodies, and their eyes were beginning to bulge. There was a thunderous roar and the androids were suddenly consumed in a fiery explosion.

He-Man's plan had worked! He had noticed that the androids focused all their attention on Grayskull, ignoring everything but a direct attack. Guessing that this meant that Hordak had only programmed them to lay siege to the castle, He-Man had instructed the Sorceress to cast her invisibility spell. With Grayskull seemingly no longer there, the androids were unable to fulfil their controller's commands, and were forced to self-destruct.

Pleased with himself, He-Man strode over to where Rio Blast and Teela lay on the ground. But before he could reach his friends he was hoisted into the air and thrown to the ground!

Wiping sand and dirt from his eyes, He-Man turned and saw that one of the androids was still functioning. "You're a tough one," he grinned, pulling back his power sword and throwing it at the giant robot. The sword streaked through the air and knocked the android over. Its heavy mechanical body fell to the ground, and finally lay still.

As He-Man retrieved his sword, Grayskull re-materialised behind him. The Sorceress was standing on the battlements and she looked down at her heroic champion and said, "It seems you have foiled yet another of Hordak's evil schemes."

"Yes," He-Man replied, "but I always seem to be battling lackeys and machines. Just for once I'd like to meet Hordak face to face!"

"Perhaps one day you will, mighty warrior," the Sorceress said. "Perhaps one day you will."

He-Man revived Teela and Rio, and the three Heroic Warriors journeyed back to the Royal Palace.

As they landed their flying craft in the courtyard, King Randor and Darill ran out to meet them.

"Did you destroy them? Did you destroy the androids?" Darill shouted.

"Yes, we did," He-Man said. "Thanks to you!"

"Yeah!" Rio exclaimed. "If not for your warning, who knows what might have happened!"

"You're to become a page boy here next year, aren't you?" Teela asked Darill, walking closer to the boy.

"Yes," Darill replied, "only..."

"Go on boy, speak your mind," King Randor said.

"Well, it's just that sometimes a year seems like forever," Darill said nervously.

"Yes, I suppose it does," Randor said. "Perhaps you would like to start your training immediately?"

"Immediately? Wow!" Darill cried, momentarily forgetting himself.

Despite the danger that had so narrowly been averted, King Randor allowed himself a faint smile...

NAME: EXTENDAR

HEIGHT: Varies between 1·83 and 4·88 metres

WEIGHT: 88·9 kilograms

EYES: Blue

HAIR: None

GROUP AFFILIATION: The Heroic Warriors

CHARACTER PROFILE: Extendar was an athlete called Doodon who was captured and experimented on by Hordak. After the experiments were finished the handsome blond-haired, blue-eyed Eternian had been transformed into a half-metal size-changing cyborg.

Extendar has the ability to extend his neck over two metres and he can stretch out his legs to a length that enables him to vault barns and other small buildings.

His closest friend was another athlete called Theydon. He too fell foul of Hordak and was also changed into a cyborg. It was Hordak's intention to force the duo to join his Horde, but Extendar managed to throw off the evil fiend's mind control and escape.

He has now joined the Heroic Warriors and has sworn not to rest until Theydon is freed from Hordak's grasp.

NAME: DRAGSTOR

HEIGHT: 1·8 metres

WEIGHT: 90 kilograms

EYES: Brown

HAIR: None

GROUP AFFILIATION: The Evil Horde

CHARACTER PROFILE: In Hordak's laboratory Theydon, Eternia's fastest sprinter, was transformed into a vicious speed demon called Dragstor.

By simply releasing his chest-wheel and starting his back-mounted turbo boosters, Dragstor can change himself into an evil warrior vehicle. In this form he likes nothing better than chasing down helpless victims and dragging them back to the Fright Zone.

Unlike his companion Extendar, Dragstor was unable to break free of the Evil Horde and is now blindly loyal to Hordak. He is the most ruthless and cunning of all Horde members. He remembers nothing of the friendship he once felt towards Extendar.

BAT ATTACK

Trailing fiery comet tails across the heavens, two meteorites hurtled through the ice-cold vastness of outer space. Travelling at unimaginable speeds, they neared the blue-green world of Eternia. Then, as if guided by some unseen hand, they veered wildly and streaked down towards the planet's surface.

On breaking cloud cover, they lost momentum and descended gracefully to the perfectly kept lawns surrounding Eternos Palace. There was a hiss of escaping air, and the meteors suddenly cracked open and elegantly unfolded, revealing themselves to be the Comet Warriors, Stonedar and Rokkon.

With slow, surprisingly delicate movements, Stonedar rose to his full height and yawned. It was only then that he noticed the palace's shattered windows. "Rokkon," he said, with mounting apprehension, "look..."

"Hmm, it's not like King Randor to allow Eternos to fall into disrepair," Rokkon said, thoughtfully. "And it is rather quiet. You don't think...?"

Not another word passed between the two friends. Instead, they silently raced towards the palace. Once inside, their worst suspicions were confirmed. The palace had fallen to a surprise attack. But how? Today was Queen Marlena's

birthday and Heroic Warriors from all across Eternia were to have gathered at the palace. They would have easily possessed enough firepower to repel any invader. Wouldn't they?

Still refusing to voice their fear, the two Comet Warriors quickly made their way to the banqueting hall. Taking the lead, Stonedar pushed open the ornately carved wooden doors.

"By the moons of Eternia!" he cried at the sight that greeted him.

"What? What is it?" Rokkon shouted, pushing past his friend and sovereign leader. "Oh my..."

Rokkon's words trailed off, his legs turned to jelly and he tried to turn away, but couldn't. Like a moth drawn to a flame, he was mesmerized by the appalling scene of destruction displayed before him. The banqueting table had been over-turned and food strewn across the room. Beautifully woven tapestries had been ripped

and shredded. And the Heroic Warriors, dazed and confused, stumbled helplessly across the littered floor.

"Ohhhh," a voice rose from the mound of bodies. It was He-Man.

Striding across to the far side of the room, Rokkon helped his friend to his feet. "Are you okay?" he said, with obvious concern.

"Yeah. I'm just a little groggy," He-Man said, rubbing the back of his head. He looked about himself, and sighed. "The room's a bit of a mess."

"You can say that again," Stonedar said, joining He-Man and Rokkon. "But how did it get like this?!"

"Well, that's kind of a long story," He-Man said. Then, after taking a deep breath, he informed the Comet Warriors of the dramatic struggle that had taken place at Eternos Palace.

The tale was quickly told, and half an hour

later, things were beginning to return to normal. Stretching, He-Man turned to Stonedar and said, "The bat-creatures obviously departed in search of richer spoils. But what I don't understand is, where did they come from?"

"Well, I've been thinking about that, and I might be able to shed a little light on the subject," Stonedar said, with a grim expression. "As you know, Rokkon and I have been visiting our homeworld, and while flying back to Eternia, our sensors picked up a peculiar series of radio waves being transmitted from the planet's surface. At the time we paid them little attention, but maybe the radio waves were actually a beacon of some kind, designed to draw the bat-creatures to Eternia!"

"NO!"

As one, He-Man and Stonedar spun around and stared in horrid fascination at Queen Marlena. She was standing in the banqueting hall's doorway, and was desperately clutching at her neck. Her glazed expression suggested she was still confused.

"My lady? What is it?" He-Man asked.

"I-It's gone," the queen croaked, still clawing at her neck.

"What's gone?"

"My I-locket. It contained a holo-pic of King Randor and Prince Adam. But...but it was from Earth! It was all I managed to salvage from my wrecked spacecraft, when I crash-landed on Eternia. And they've taken it. The bat-creatures have taken it!"

This was the final indignity! Without warning the bat-creatures had invaded Eternia. They had struck out at random, and caused all manner of havoc and destruction. And, while she lay unconscious, they had stolen Queen Marlena's

most treasured possession. He-Man had had enough! "Stonedar," he whispered, through tightly clenched teeth, "this beacon you spoke of earlier, can you trace it back to its source?"

"Er...yes," Stonedar said, unsure of He-Man's intentions.

"Good," He-Man said, striding stealthily towards the doorway. "Because you, Rokkon and I are going to pay a visit to whoever's responsible for all this carnage!"

"Don't you think we should take along some of the other Heroic Warriors?" Rokkon asked.

"No. They're probably still too groggy from the bat-creatures' attack. Besides, considering the mood I'm in right now, I don't think I'll need much back-up!"

The heroes were soon on their way, Eternos Palace fading to a tiny dot behind them. Rokkon and Stonedar were once more in their meteor

forms, and He-Man was sitting behind the wheel of the armour plated Attak Trak. His eyes were dark, narrow slits and his expression unreadable.

"As far as I can tell, the beacon's coming from this direction," Stonedar shouted down to He-Man, as he streaked past the Attak Trak with an ear-splitting roar.

For hour after long hour, across mile upon endless mile, the three friends followed the radio wave trail. All about them they saw the terrible destruction wrought by the bat-creatures. Trees, some nearly as old as Castle Grayskull, had been violently torn from the soft earth and scattered across the landscape. Entire wheat fields had been cut down and trampled on, and orchards stripped of their fruit. Practically a whole year's harvest had been destroyed in a single day. Rationing would be necessary for the next few months, and it would take many years for the

Eternian farmers to recover from the attack, and make up the short-fall.

With such sobering thoughts in mind, the group passed through the now desolate farming region and into the treacherous sun-baked area, situated close to the Mountains of Mourne. Dotted about the craggy slopes, they could clearly see hundreds, perhaps thousands, of the bat-creatures. They were crouching on their haunches and their blood-red eyes were wide and seemingly alert. However, despite initial appearances, they were unmoving and fast asleep.

"We'd best proceed with caution from now on," He-Man said quietly. "I don't want to take on those monsters before we find the source of the beacon."

"Speaking of the beacon," Stonedar said, slowly. "It seems the radio waves are being emitted from somewhere in the next valley. And I don't think you need me to remind you what's down there..."

"Snake Mountain," He-Man whispered, his eyes widening. Then, snarling through clenched teeth, he said, "It was Skeletor – ALL ALONG, IT WAS SKELETOR!"

In a blazing rage, he turned the Attak Trak into the valley and towards Snake Mountain. Pushing violently at the buttons that controlled the vehicle's weapons systems, he fired a barrage of laser beams at Skeletor's foul, mist-covered lair. With a splintering of wood and the shattering of metal supports, the fortress' ancient door disintegrated. Slamming the Attak Trak into a skid, He-Man leapt, panther-like, into the gloomy fortress.

It was empty.

Transforming into their humanoid forms, Rokkon and Stonedar soon followed He-Man into Snake Mountain. Together the three friends began to scour the evil fortress in search of Skeletor and his cronies. Eventually they stumbled across a trapdoor, sunken into the basement floor. There was no visible handle, and so He-Man dug his broad fingers into the tiny gap between the wooden planks and the stone flaggings. Then, mustering his mighty strength, he prised it open.

Beneath the trapdoor lay a flight of stone steps. For the most part, they were covered in a thick coat of dust and grime. But this had been disturbed in places, as if someone had recently used the gloomy stairwell. Certain that they were on the right track, the Heroic Warriors descended

into the darkness. Minutes later, they found themselves standing in a subterranean cave, located deep beneath Snake Mountain. Ahead of them lay an ancient wooden door. He-Man raised his Power Sword and fired a bolt of electricity at it. The soft, rotten timbers began to smoulder and burn through.

On the opposite side of the door Beast Man, who was supposedly standing guard, but was actually dozing, leapt backwards and yelped, "Skeletor! Skeletor!"

"Yes, Beast Man?" Skeletor said, emerging from a dank slime-encrusted tunnel. "What is it?"

"It's me, Skeletor!" He-Man shouted, as he and the Comet Warriors finally broke through the door.

Reacting almost instinctively, Skeletor raised his ram's-head staff and fired a magical power blast at the Eternian heroes. The blast sped towards its targets, but it merely bounced off

Stonedar's rough, rocky outer shell.

The sound of the deflected force blast echoed throughout the network of twisting tunnels, attracting the attention of Whiplash, Spikor and the other evil warriors. Soon they were locked in close combat with He-Man and his companions. However, from his vantage point on the edge of the battle, Skeletor could see that, despite their superior numbers, his cronies were hopelessly outmatched. They would lose. They always lost – but this time they wouldn't drag him down with them!

Racing through the series of underground caves, Skeletor made his way to his radio wave transmitter. Then, stooping low, he increased the machine's frequency. This caused bat-creatures from across all of Eternia to converge on Snake Mountain. They entered the fortress, found their way to the underground caves, and attacked the battling heroes and villains.

Unable to resist temptation, Skeletor returned to the battle-site in order to taunt his mortal enemy one last time. "You're finished, He-Man! FINISHED!" he cackled. Then, using his magical powers, he teleported himself out of Snake Mountain.

With their leader's departure, the evil warriors lost the will to fight, and they scurried off into the deepest corners of the underground caves. Behind them, He-Man and the Comet Warriors were left to contend with the savage bat-creatures.

"This is useless!" Stonedar said, turning to Rokkon. "The only way to defeat these winged demons is by disposing of the beacon."

"Yes, you're right," Rokkon said, and together the two Comet Warriors hunted down the radio transmitter. They managed to drag it to the surface and then, carrying it between them, they soared skyward.

With an inhuman shriek the bat-creatures flew after them, automatically following the signals that were still being sent out by the transmitter. Only just managing to stay ahead of the howling pack, Stonedar and Rokkon soon reached deep space. Using all their alien-born strength they threw the transmitter into the inky, black void. The bat-creatures followed it and Eternia was finally free of their dreaded scourge.

BAT ATTACK EPILOGUE

Queen Marlena was sitting in her bedchamber. Many days had passed since Stonedar and Rokkon had saved the planet from the bat-creatures, yet she still refused to leave the confines of the palace. Her heart was heavy, her mood sad.

There was a knock at the door and Prince Adam entered the room. "Hello Mother," he said, tentatively.

Refusing to meet her son's gaze, the queen said, "We lost this time, didn't we, Adam? Skeletor's plan caused so much destruction. Things will never be the same again."

"We didn't win, but I don't think we lost," Adam said. "Here, He-Man asked me to give you this. Apparently he tore it from the neck of one of the bat-creatures he fought beneath

Snake Mountain." Adam took hold of his mother's hand and placed something small and metallic inside it. He closed her fingers about the tiny object and left the room.

As the door clicked shut behind her son, Marlena opened her fist.

Inside it was her beloved locket.

It was scratched and tarnished and the chain had been broken. But, despite the damage it was still whole – still repairable. And, with a smile, Marlena realized that the spirit of the Eternian heroes was also repairable. The forces of good had come close to defeat but, with the power of the Elders, they had survived. Soon, their strength would be renewed and, on one glorious day in the future, they would finally beat the forces of evil.

NAME: STONEDAR

HEIGHT: 2·13 metres

WEIGHT: 500 kilograms

EYES: Granite

HAIR: None

STONEDAR

GROUP AFFILIATION: The Heroic Warriors

CHARACTER PROFILE: Stonedar is a living-rock creature and he is the leader of an alien race known as the Comet People. His world was a peaceful planet, free from hunger and wars...at least it was until the Evil Horde arrived!

Using an orbiting satellite known as an 'energy-stealer', Hordak lay siege to the Comet World, threatening to destroy it and all its inhabitants. However, unknown to Hordak, Stonedar and his people have the ability to transform themselves into living meteors, and in this mighty form they were able to soar through the vacuum of space and destroy the evil satellite.

After repelling Hordak's attack Stonedar swore an oath to battle against the Evil Horde anywhere in the universe.

ROKKON

NAME: ROKKON

HEIGHT: 1·98 metres

WEIGHT: 467 kilograms

EYES: Quartz

HAIR: None

GROUP AFFILIATION: The Heroic Warriors

CHARACTER PROFILE: Considerably younger than Stonedar, Rokkon exhibits all the rashness of youth. After hearing of his companion's vow to fight against the Evil Horde, it was he who convinced the Comet leader that they should both travel to Eternia.

On reaching King Randor's beautiful world, the duo naturally joined the Heroic Warriors, and now they not only battle against the forces of Hordak but also those of Skeletor and King Hiss.

Like all Comet People, Rokkon can travel through space while in his meteor form. He navigates by sonic waves and can fly at almost light speed. His outer shell is incredibly tough and can withstand many laser blasts.

TRIVIA TEST

Things are really hotting up on Eternia! Hordak has expanded his Evil Horde, the Snake Men have returned, and the ranks of the Heroic Warriors swell almost daily. What with new heroes, new villains and now three evil forces, things can get a little confusing. Despite this, the Heroic Warrior needs an in-depth knowledge of his allies, his enemies and his enemies' enemies. Do *you* possess such a knowledge? Why not take my Masters of the Universe Trivia Test and find out?

Each question is on a specific topic, and is divided into three parts, **a**, **b** and **c**. All three parts must be answered in sequence. A correct answer to part **a** of a question means you score 4 points and can go on to part **b**. A correct answer to part **b** means you score an additional 6 points and can proceed to part **c**. Answer part **c** correctly and you score another 10 points, making your total score for one whole question 20 points. If you answer part **a** incorrectly you *cannot* go on to parts **b** and **c**, and must proceed to part **a** of the next question. If you have answered part **a** correctly, but have failed to answer part **b**, you *cannot* proceed to part **c**. You must go directly to the *next question*.

If you have failed to answer all three parts of a question, your score is nil. If you have answered part **a**, your score is 4 points. If you have answered parts **a** and **b**, your score is 10 points. Check your answers and overall score rating on the following page.

Question One

a) What is the name of Skeletor's evil lair? (4 pts)
b) Skeletor can often be seen riding into battle on the back of a great cat. What is it called? (6 pts)
c) Skeletor comes from which planet? (10 pts)

Question Two

a) Who is the Guardian of Castle Grayskull? (4 pts)
b) Rokkon and Stonedar are members of which alien race? (6 pts)
c) The Avions are the Birdpeople of Eternia. Who is their leader? (10 pts)

Question Three

a) Which area of Eternia is under Horde control? (4 pts)
b) Hordak is leader of the Evil Horde, but who is Hordak's commander? (6 pts)
c) Hordak is responsible for the creation of which two Heroic Warriors? (10 pts)

Question Four

a) How is Adora related to Prince Adam? (4 pts)
b) King Randor is a native of the planet Eternia, but where does his wife, Queen Marlena, come from? (6 pts)
c) He-Man's sword is called the Sword of Power. By what name is She-Ra's sword known? (10 pts)

Question Five

a) Who cast King Hiss and the Snake Men into an alien dimension? (4 pts)
b) How many Snake Men are there? (6 pts)
c) One of the Snake Men also works for Skeletor. Is it Snake Face, Rattlor or Kobra Khan? (10 pts)

Question Six

a) When he draws his sword Adam changes into He-Man. Who does Cringer change into? (4 pts)
b) Excluding the Sorceress, which three Heroic Warriors are aware of He-Man's secret identity? (6 pts)
c) The Thunderpunch, the Lightning Leap or Superbreath. Which one of these attributes did the Sorceress bestow on He-Man? (10pts)

Answers

Question One
a) Snake Mountain   b) Panthor   c) Infinita

Question Two
a) The Sorceress   b) The Comet People   c) Stratos

Question Three
a) The Fright Zone   b) Horde Prime   c) Snout Spout and Extendar

Question Four
a) She is his twin sister   b) Earth   c) The Sword of Protection

Question Five
a) The Elders   b) Thousands (although only five are now active on Eternia)   c) Kobra Khan

Question Six
a) Battle Cat   b) Battle Cat, Orko and Man-At-Arms   c) The Thunderpunch

All finished? Good. Now compare your total score with these ratings.

0–20: Hmm...I'm afraid you've done rather poorly. But don't worry, an in-depth reading of this book will certainly increase your Masters knowledge!

21–70: This is more like it. You've got a good working knowledge of the forces of good and evil. If you continue to show an interest in all things Eternian, you'll soon become an expert on the Masters of the Universe.

71–120: Well done! You seem to know as much about Eternia as I do. Why don't you catch the next Space Warp here, and take up the battle against Skeletor and Hordak? The Heroic Warriors and I could do with a rest!

A FRIEND IN NEED...

As it had so often happened in the past, the courtyard of Eternos Palace rang to the clamour of battle. It was all heard once again – the distinctive hum of laser fire, the grunting and wheezing of warriors, the shrill chime of metal striking metal. Yet this time it wasn't the sound of Eternian Heroes grappling with evil foes, but the sound of Heroic Warriors struggling against their fellows. The sound of Man-At-Arms and Extendar battling with Stonedar and Rokkon.

Man-At-Arms steadied himself, wiping sweat from his eyes with the back of his hand. Stonedar was bearing down on him and he slowly raised his megalaser, aimed it, and fired a stream of violet light pulses at the advancing Comet Warrior. The shimmering energy blasts sped towards their target, crashing into Stonedar's outer shell. But they merely caused him to stagger backwards, and he quickly regained his balance.

Then, after transforming into his meteor form, he propelled himself at the Eternian scientist. There was little time for retreat and Man-At-Arms was bowled over, and dumped on the cobblestone floor. Stonedar was looming above him. The leader of the Comet People had reverted to his humanoid form and was grinning, smugly. With speed, uncommon in a man of his age, Man-At-Arms suddenly rolled onto his side and lashed out with his legs, tripping Stonedar.

The full weight of the mightly alien space warrior smashed to the ground, cracking the cobblestones. He slowly picked himself up. "It'll take a lot more than a fall to knock me out of commission," he said, with a smile.

"Oh, I know it will," came a voice from behind the Comet Person. Stonedar quickly turned, but was caught and held fast by the steel-strong arms of Extendar.

"Hang on, Stonedar!" cried Rokkon, racing across the courtyard towards his companion. He grasped Extendar's arms and tried to break the fierce grip he had on his friend. On seeing this, Man-At-Arms scrambled to his feet and hurled himself at Rokkon, adding to the already chaotic struggle. For long, silent minutes the battle continued and then, without warning, the four Heroic Warriors fell to the ground, landing in a confusing mass of flailing limbs.

"I see you're enjoying yourselves," laughed Prince Adam, as he left Eternos Palace and strolled across the courtyard. "But I'm afraid I'll have to put a stop to your antics! The time allocated for your training session has run out."

"Already? I don't believe it!" exclaimed Man-At-Arms, rubbing a sore and bruised shoulder.

"Never mind, Man-At-Arms," said Stonedar, standing, "maybe you and Extendar will get the better of Rokkon and I next time."

"NEXT TIME! What do you mean 'NEXT TIME'? We won THIS combat!"

"Ha, ha, ha! I don't think so!" laughed

Stonedar, transforming into his meteor form and soaring skyward. "Come on Rokkon...What d'you say to a relaxing flight through the upper atmosphere?"

"Sounds good to me!" replied Rokkon, joining his friend in the air. The two Comet People climbed higher and higher. Soon they were nothing but distant, grey-coloured specks. Then they were gone.

"How do those two do it? Don't they ever rest?" asked Man-At-Arms, turning to Adam.

"Who knows?" replied the prince, with a shrug of his shoulders. "Anyway such commitment is vital if we're ever to defeat the forces of evil!"

"Of course it is lad!" said Man-At-Arms placing a friendly hand on Adam's shoulder. "And I wasn't complaining! Now why don't we take a trip to my laboratory. There's a couple of new weapons systems I've been meaning to show you."

Together the two friends turned, walked briskly across the courtyard, and entered Eternos Palace. Behind them, Extendar looked down at the broken cobblestones and sighed, wearily. He was alone. He seemed always to be alone.

Since arriving at the Royal Palace, he'd been made more than welcome. But the Heroic Warriors were a tightly knit band, and Extendar had been somehow excluded from the group. Prince Adam, Man-At-Arms, even Stonedar and Rokkon – they all seemed to prefer the company of a few long-established friends. Friends with whom they shared common bonds of loyalty and fellowship. Extendar just hadn't known the Eternian heroes long enough to establish such bonds, and the last time he had experienced true friendship was when he was still known as Doodon, the athlete. His closest companion then had been a fellow athlete, Theydon. The pair were virtually inseparable. They ran races together, organized sporting events and generally enjoyed each other's company. But on one fateful day, they accidentally crossed the border into the Fright Zone and were captured by Hordak. He transformed them into the cyborg-warriors, Extendar and Dragstor. However, with a supreme effort of will, Extendar had managed to throw off the effects of Hordak's mind control and escape – but not so Dragstor. All traces of Theydon's former personality had been removed. He had been turned into a mindless automaton, blindly loyal to Hordak and the Evil Horde.

He-Man had vowed to help free the brainwashed Dragstor, yet all his attempts to do

so had met with failure. And now, with almost daily attacks from Skeletor and King Hiss, it seemed unlikely that he'd have the time to fulfil his oath. No, if anyone was going to free Dragstor it was Extendar, and with this thought in mind he extended his legs to their fullest length, strode over the palace battlements, and began to march across the green plains of Eternia. Many miles ahead of him lay the dark side of the planet. And, beyond that, the Fright Zone.

For three long years the Fright Zone had been a safe sanctuary to the Evil Horde. After travelling from Etheria to Eternia, Hordak had wasted little time in selecting a vast area of many square kilometres to serve as his new home. Then, using his arcane science, he had moulded it into an exact replica of the Etherian Fright Zone. With a casualness bordering on contempt, he transformed an area of great natural beauty into a charred and blasted landscape. Acre after acre of grass was scorched, and turned into black, infertile ash. Rivers were dammed and filled, creating deep and treacherous marshes. And tall, ancient trees were set ablaze – reduced to little more than brittle husks.

This transformation had resulted in all animal life fleeing the area. No birds were seen nesting in the trees, no stallions roaming the meadows. In fact, the only sound to be heard was that made by the swarms of bats, introduced to the region by Hordak. Not surprisingly, the Fright Zone's infamous reputation had preceded it and it was now avoided by all good Eternians.

Still, Extendar was well aware of such facts, and undaunted, he continued on his journey. Many hours after leaving Eternos he entered Hordak's nightmare land. He peered into the gloom. Hordak's lair was located at the heart of the Fright Zone, but Extendar had no idea in which direction this lay. No matter where he looked, everything appeared to be the same – as if the entire region had been purposely designed to confuse travellers. With a sinking feeling in the pit of his stomach, Extendar realized he was lost.

Still, at least on his way to the Fright Zone, he'd had enough time to plan how he was going to free Dragstor. This time there would be no cunning ploys, no stalking in the darkness. This time he'd simply march up to Hordak and offer to surrender – on the condition Dragstor was immediately released and dispatched to Eternos Palace. Extendar realized that if his madcap scheme succeeded he'd face torture and worse. But it was a small price to pay for the freedom of his friend.

With renewed determination, Extendar increased the length of his telescopic neck so that he could peer above the tree-tops. To the east he could see the smoke of a camp fire. It was undoubtedly the Evil Horde's base and, after memorizing its precise location, Extendar returned to his normal proportions.

Suddenly there was a clap of thunder and Extendar was struck by a silver-blue blast of electricity. He staggered and fell forward, into a pool of bubbling mud. Pulling himself free from the oozing swamp, he turned and stared at his attacker. It was Hordak.

"Unless you want another blast from this," the evil scientist sneered, aiming an electro-shock pistol at Extendar, "I suggest you remain perfectly still!"

"H-How did you know I was here?" Extendar gasped.

"Oh, you're so naive, Extendar! My orbiting satellite sighted you as soon as you entered the Fright Zone."

As if on cue, the ape-like Grizzlor shambled out of a dense thicket of burned-out trees. He turned to Hordak and said, "Shall I bind the Heroic fool, master?"

"No!" Extendar cried. "There's no need – I came here to strike a bargain."

"A bargain, eh?" Hordak said, thoughtfully.

"Yes. You free Dragstor and I'll give myself up!"

"Ha, ha, ha! And what made you think I'd honour such a bargain?" laughed Hordak. "Right now both you and Dragstor are in my power. And that's how things are going to stay! Grizzlor, take him."

"WHERE IS HE? He can't just have disappeared off the face of Eternia!" shouted Prince Adam, as he paced the stone battlements of Eternos Palace. Unusually silent, his friend and pet, Cringer, padded alongside him. Extendar's absence had been noticed, and for some hours now the other Heroic Warriors had been out looking for their missing comrade. Adam and Cringer had remained behind to co-ordinate the numerous search parties but as yet, they'd heard nothing. Understandably, they were growing increasingly restless.

"Relax, Adam," Cringer said, "Extendar will turn up...I hope!"

Suddenly, Moss Man appeared on the battlements. "Adam!" he cried, "I've been communicating telepathically with the trees in the Evergreen Forest and they say that Extendar passed by them over four hours ago. He was heading westward."

"Westward? There's nothing in that direction except..." Adam suddenly paused, realization sinking in, "EXCEPT THE FRIGHT ZONE! Come on Cringer! If Extendar's gone there...there's no telling what trouble he's in!"

The great cat and the Prince of the Eternian Realm raced from Eternos Palace, and sped across the royal gardens. Once out of sight, Adam drew his power sword. With a blinding flash of magical energy, Adam was transformed into He-Man and Cringer into Battle Cat. He-Man leapt on to the back of his mighty steed and, with grim determination, the pair headed westward.

Hours later the amazing duo reached the boundary of the Fright Zone. Dismounting, He-Man raised his sword and fired a pencil thin beam of energy skyward. Travelling at the speed of light, the beam soared up through the outer atmosphere and struck the Horde's spy satellite, destroying it in a fiery explosion.

Free from Hordak's prying gaze, He-Man and Battle Cat quickly made their way to the centre of the Horde encampment. Leech, Modulok and the other Horde warriors were huddled in a small group, whispering. Occasionally they cast furtive glances at the Eternian heroes, but they made no

move to stop them.

"By Horde Prime! I don't believe you, He-Man. How dare you confront me here on my own territory!" Hordak cried, darting out of a small wicker hut.

"Let's get straight to the point, Hordak," He-Man said, calmly. "I'm here to challenge you to personal combat. If I win, both Extendar and Dragstor return to Eternos with me. If you're the victor you can dispose of me as you will."

Hordak fell silent. Personal combat was an ancient tradition, designed to allow individual Horde members the opportunity to honourably settle their differences. Hordak had, in fact, risen to his current position by confronting and defeating his enemies in such contests. Still, He-Man wasn't a Horde member and Hordak was under no obligation to accept the challenge. If he didn't, however, he'd lose face in front of his

troops. Leech and the others would take refusal to fight as a sign of weakness, and then they would be harder to control in the future. But it would be even more difficult to keep them in line if he accepted the challenge and lost!

Hordak lowered his head, carefully considering his options. Minutes later he looked up and stared hard at He-Man. "Very well," he said, "Modulok, fetch this fool a weapon."

Modulok disappeared into a hut and returned moments later carrying a bizarre weapon. He threw it at He-Man's feet.

"Ah, a three-headed mighty mace," He-Man said admiringly. "I haven't used one of these in a long time." He stooped and picked up the weapon. It was basically an armband, with three metal spokes attached to it. The spokes ended in heavy, golden-coloured balls. He-Man strapped the contraption to his forearm and clenched his

fist. In response, the spokes began to spin at an incredible speed.

"Well, I've my weapon," He-Man said to Hordak. "What are you going to use?"

"Oh, I'll think of something!" Hordak exclaimed, suddenly transforming his arm into a photon cannon, and blasting the Heroic Warrior.

He-Man was slammed backwards. "I take it the combat's started, then?" he said, leaping at his evil foe.

Preparing himself for the attack, Hordak raised his cannon arm and, with the distinctive whir of working machinery, a three-headed thunderball mace sprouted from its barrel.

CLANG! With a sound that echoed throughout the entire Fright Zone, the two enemies clashed in deadly combat. He-Man spun his mace at Hordak's chest, but the Horde Commander leapt backwards, skilfully avoiding the blow.

"Ugghhh," He-Man gasped, falling forward on to his knees.

Hordak bent low and said, "Before I came to this pitiful mudball of a planet, I used to be known as Hurricane Hordak. Do you know why? It's because I smashed everything in my path!"

With an evil chuckle he swung his mace at the Eternian. But He-Man miraculously darted out of the way, and scrambled to his feet.

"It's time this game ended," He-Man said, delivering a crushing blow. He struck out with the mighty mace a second time.

Defenceless against He-Man's furious assault, Hordak crumbled and fell to the ground. "Stop! Stop!" he begged. "You win...YOU WIN!"

"You're so noble in defeat, Hordak," He-Man said, sarcastically. "Now where are Extendar and Dragstor?"

Hordak turned to his evil friends. "M-Modulok, L-Leech, go and f-fetch Extendar and Dragstor," he whimpered.

Soon, a much relieved Extendar was standing beside He-Man. "Boy am I glad to see you!" he said. "I was sure Hordak was going to use his Slime Pit to turn me into a Slime Monster!"

"Well you're safe now," He-Man said. "And both you and Dragstor are coming home with me."

At this Dragstor, who had been standing close to Extendar turned and walked over to Hordak. He seemed worried and puzzled, and he took a deep breath of the fuel vapours that travelled down the cables attached to the side of his head unit. Inside the steel casing of his body, his powerful engines revved and stopped...revved and stopped.

"It's all right, Dragstor," Hordak said, almost gently, "you can go with them."

And so, a short while later, He-Man and Battle Cat, along with Extendar and Dragstor left the Fright Zone on their way back to Eternos Palace.

"It was terrible," Extendar said, obviously shaken by his experience. "Just terrible! I was chained to a cold stone wall and..."

"It's okay," He-Man said, reassuringly. "Once we're back at Eternos you'll be able to enjoy a well deserved rest."

Eternos. At the sound of this single word, Dragstor stopped dead in his tracks. Although he'd been fitted with only limited intelligence circuits, he knew that Eternos was home to Hordak's enemies. But why had Hordak ordered him to go there? It just didn't make sense. Hordak must have been mistaken. But even if this was the case, could Dragstor disobey a direct command? Yes he could! And, displaying independent thought for the first time since he was transformed into a cyborg, he turned and sped back to the Fright Zone. Back to his master, Hordak. Back to his only friend!

"Dragstor! Stop!" Extendar cried after him. "You don't know that you're doing! Stop!"

"Let him go," He-Man said softly. "We'll never catch him now. Besides, it's probably best this way. We might not have been able to reverse the effects of Hordak's mind control. And who knows what might have happened then? No, if Dragstor is ever to truly escape the Evil Horde, he'll have to leave them of his own free will."

"Yes, I suppose you're right," Extendar said, with a heavy heart. And, with his two friends beside him, he began the long journey back to the Royal Palace of Eternos.

50

NAME: THE SNAKE MEN

BASE OF OPERATIONS: Viper Tower

KNOWN ALLIES: Skeletor

KNOWN ENEMIES: All Mankind

PROFILE: Sssssss! Bolt your doors. Bar your windows. The dreaded Snake Men have returned, and this time they're here to stay! Centuries ago, thousands of warrior Snake Men invaded Eternia. They spread out across the beautiful blue-green world, conquering everything in their path. Seemingly unstoppable, the repulsive reptiles built two fortresses, Snake Mountain and Viper Tower, from which to plan their war effort. However,

their victory was only short lived, as the Elders quickly mustered their magical strength and cast them into an alien dimension. The entire Snake Army languished in this timeless realm for hundreds of years, until Skeletor learned of their existence, and tried to use his powers to bring them back across the dimensional planes. However, such a task proved too great for the Master of Evil, and he was only able to transport five Snake Men to Eternia. These five are:

KING HISS

King Hiss is the leader of the Snake Men. At first glance he appears to be a young, handsome Heroic Warrior, but when his outer skin is peeled back, his true identity as a hideous five-headed snake creature is revealed!

TUNG LASHOR

Second only to King Hiss in strength and cunning, Tung Lashor is able to paralyse his foes with a quick lick of his incredibly long tongue. He is also able to spray magical venom, which sets within seconds, trapping his luckless victim inside an unbreakable shell. Tung Lashor has an unusual sense of humour, and he likes to lash his tongue at his fellow Snake Men just to shake them up once in a while!

SSSQUEEZE

Sssqueeze is rather slow and dim-witted and is always being ordered about by the other Snake Men. His unbelievably long arms are incredibly powerful, and he's able to wrap them around his foes, squeezing them until they're unconscious.

SNAKE FACE

Although he appears quiet and timid, Snake Face is not one to be crossed. He is the Snake Men's greatest warrior and is skilled with every imaginable weapon, particularly mace and shield. He's also a master of unarmed combat and can easily hold his own against any three foes.

RATTLOR

Tung Lashor's best friend is Rattlor, although what the two find to talk about no one knows, as Rattlor prefers hissing to speaking. This silence gives him a mysterious, eerie quality, which he uses to great effect in combat. Just before he strikes, however, he will sound his battle rattle, giving his victim a tiny fraction of a second to realize their horrible fate.

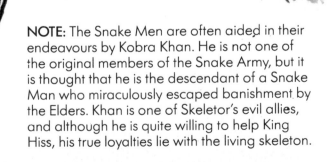

NOTE: The Snake Men are often aided in their endeavours by Kobra Khan. He is not one of the original members of the Snake Army, but it is thought that he is the descendant of a Snake Man who miraculously escaped banishment by the Elders. Khan is one of Skeletor's evil allies, and although he is quite willing to help King Hiss, his true loyalties lie with the living skeleton.

Weather Wizardry

Slowly, winter slackened its ice-cold grip on the magical world of Eternia...releasing it into the warmth of spring, and then summer. Across the planet flowers bloomed, animals awoke from hibernation, and people from all walks of life found themselves unconsciously whistling along to the morning chorus of birdsong. Even the most business-like agreed that it was a time of renewal. Of rest and relaxation...

"Ah, this is lovely," Teela sighed, gliding dolphin-like through the crisp, cool waters of one of the many rivers found in the Evergreen Forest. "Just lovely."

"Humph, I don't really understand what you humans see in swimming," Cringer muttered, from where he was lying on the grassy bank. "It gets you all wet!"

"Ha, ha. Of course it gets you wet," Teela laughed, treading water. "And considering how hot it is right now, I'd say that was a blessing."

"Well, I agree with Cringer," Orko said, suddenly materializing in the air above Teela. "We Trollans never let water touch our bodies."

"B-but how do you wash yourselves?" Teela said, vainly trying to hide the surprise in her voice.

"How do we wash ourselves? That's easy...we use magic to keep clean."

"Ha! And we all know how reliable your magic is!" Cringer shouted, as he lazily turned onto his side.

"Cringer! Don't be so rude!" Teela cried. Then, sweeping her arm in a great arc, she sent a torrent of water cascading onto the river bank.

With a high pitched yelp, Cringer leapt

54

a bathing costume."

"Bathing costume? Oh, I don't think I'd suit one of those...besides I don't really like swimming."

"Well I think it's simply divine," the usually matter-of-fact Captain of the Guard said, turning on to her back, closing her eyes, and sailing to the far side of the river. "Anyway, if you're not going to swim, the least you can do is remove your shirt...you must be roasting!"

"Er...no...no, not really," Adam said, wiping sweat from his eyes with the back of his hand.

"Oh, of course you're not, Adam!" Teela laughed, sarcastically. "You know, you should take a leaf out of He-Man's book...he's not afraid to show off his physique."

"Yes, well it's surprising he doesn't get sunstroke," Adam muttered. "It gets far too hot for him to run around like he does. Far too hot."

"This miserable planet just doesn't get hot enough," Tung Lashor hissed, his words barely audible in the foul, slimy interior of Viper Tower.

His fellow Snake Men were standing close by, and Snake Face and Sssqueeze murmured in agreement. Rattlor, ever silent, swung his mighty tail from side to side, enthusiastically sounding his battle-rattle. The Snake Men were cold blooded creatures, used to operating in a tropical environment, and throughout Eternia's bitter winter they had remained inside their dank, dark fortress...its heavy atmosphere offering them some degree of comfort. Now, with the arrival of summer, they would soon resume their war against the forces of Grayskull. Yet surprisingly, this prospect was greeted with little enthusiasm. Even the warmest of Eternian days were far colder than those on their home world and so long as they remained on the planet, they would always act in a slow, sluggish manner.

"It just doesn't get hot enough," Tung Lashor repeated. "Snake Men just can't function properly in this type of climate. Why King Hiss wants this mudball, I don't know!"

"I want it, because Eternia is a storehouse of potent magical energies! And as such it will make a fine cornerstone for my new galactic empire," King Hiss said, entering the room. Weeks earlier he had mysteriously locked himself in his private chambers. Now he appeared pale and drawn, as if suffering from lack of food and sleep.

"Oh master, it's so good to see you again," Sssqueeze said, darting forward, towards his sovereign leader.

backwards...and bumped into Adam, as the prince absent-mindedly strolled into the sun-drenched glade.

"Whua?" Adam murmured, as he suddenly found himself tumbling to the ground.

Flying over to the prince, Orko hovered above him and said, "Adam, are you all right?"

"I-I guess so," the prince replied, climbing to his feet, and wiping loose the leaves that had become attached to the back of his legs.

"Oh, Adam! Look at you!" Teela said, continuing to tread water. "You're still dressed in your winter clothes!"

Adam lowered his head, looked down at his white shirt, crushed velvet jerkin, and maroon leggings and said, "I am?"

"Yes, you are. For this type of weather you need

Hiss pushed him aside. "Away with you, you miserable wretch," he said. Then, staggering to the far side of the room, the leader of the Snake Men slumped onto a granite throne, covered with reptile skins. He held his head in his hands for long minutes, while the other Snake Men stared at him with apprehension.

Eventually he looked up and addressed his minions. "As you all know, by banishing us into the Timeless Dimensions, the Elders have extended our lives by millions of years. However, an unfortunate side effect of this, is that our memories are simply unable to cope with the countless experiences we have had over the years. At one time or another, we have all been unable to remember something from our past...particularly from the time of our original occupation of Eternia."

"Yeah...that's right!" Sssqueeze shouted, dim-wittedly.

"It has been my belief that our past contained some vital piece of information that would help us to finally defeat He-Man and his wretched band," King Hiss continued. "And, while you idled away your time, I have spent the last weeks in quiet contemplation, searching through the fog of my memory for this information. This morning my efforts were rewarded...WITH SUCCESS!"

"What are you talking about, Hiss?" Tung Lashor said, scornfully. "What we need to do is change this planet's climate, not waste time delving into our murky past."

It was the same expression that he wore hours later, when he found himself standing inside the ancient Pyramid of Myrabim. Open-mouthed, he was staring at the device Hiss had spoken of. It was large and metallic, shaped like a laser cannon, balanced on an enormous steel-rimmed support stand. Attached to the back of the stand, there was a padded control chair. According to Hiss, the whole contraption was called a weather cannon. Apparently it had been invented thousands of years ago, by the Elders' Eternian scientists. It was their intention to use it to alter the planet's weather patterns, in an attempt to produce higher and longer lasting crop yields. However, it was never fired as the Elders thought it was too unpredictable to be used.

All this, King Hiss had coolly, calmly told Tung Lashor and the other Snake Men. Then, throwing off his tiredness as one would cast aside an old cloak, he had led his minions here to the Desert Zone...to the legend-shrouded Pyramid of Myrabim!

When the Snake Men had originally invaded Eternia, Myrabim had been the seat of the Elders' magical power. However, over the years, they had gradually moved their court to Castle Grayskull, leaving behind them many abandoned inventions.

"Is it not a fine machine?" King Hiss said,

Hiss fixed his hypnotic gaze on the strongest of his followers, and said, "How right you are, Tung Lashor."

"What? I am...?"

"Yes. While lost in meditation I remembered a device that will do just as you ask...and by doing so, it will help us conquer Eternia!"

Tung Lashor fell silent, with an embarrassed dumbfounded expression.

suddenly breaking Tung Lashor's trance. "You have to admit, the Elders knew how to build things."

With a crooked smile Hiss walked over towards the weather cannon, gently stroking its smooth metallic surface, before hoisting himself into the control seat. Then, with a sudden movement, he stabbed at a violet-coloured button situated on the arm rest.

Instantly, a stone slab in the side of the pyramid slid back. Sunlight streamed into the interior of the ancient building shining down on Tung Lashor and the other Snake Men. They hissed in obvious surprise.

Ignoring the shocked, awed cries of his minions, Hiss pressed the button a second time. A beam of white light was expelled from the barrel of the weather cannon. It soared through the gap in the pyramid's stone wall, up into the cloudless, perfectly-blue sky. For a split second, the horizon glowed a fiery red...and then...nothing.

"That's it?!" Tung Lashor cried, turning to King Hiss. "That's it? Where's the miraculous climate change you promised, Hiss? Where?"

"Be warned, Tung Lashor. You're beginning to try my temper!" Hiss said, climbing down from the weather cannon. "Besides, the beam of light you saw is already changing the chemical composition of Eternia's atmosphere. Once this process is complete the sun's rays will be stronger and the planet will slowly, but most definitely heat up. Soon, Eternia will be transformed into a tropical jungle-bound world and there's nothing the Heroic Warriors can do about it. Nothing! Ha, ha, ha!"

In the weeks that followed, everything happened as King Hiss had predicted. Temperatures across Eternia slowly rose, food crops withered and died, and farmers began to complain of water shortages. At first, Eternians thought they were merely experiencing a severe heat-wave. But as temperatures continued to soar so did suspicions. Finally King Randor asked Man-At-Arms to investigate the situation. Closeted in his laboratory, the master scientist soon discovered the reason for the dramatic change in climate. There was no time to waste. He called He-Man to his chambers.

"From my atmospheric studies, I'm convinced that someone has found and activated the Elders' ancient weather cannon," Man-At-Arms gasped, finding it difficult to breathe in the fierce, mid-day heat.

"But if I remember my history lessons correctly, there's no way to reverse the process once it's begun," He-Man said, seemingly unaware of the extremely high temperature.

"That was true when the machine was originally invented...but with recent technological advances I think I can change its polarity. Then I'll be able to fire a second beam into the atmosphere, reversing the damage done to the climate."

"Great! Well, we'd better get started...as far as I know, the weather cannon's still inside the Myrabim Pyramid, and that's located on the opposite side of the planet!"

As He-Man and Man-At-Arms went quickly out of the laboratory, a small, brownish lizard emerged from beneath a work bench. It followed the heroic duo out of the room and then left Eternos Palace. Almost half a day later, it arrived

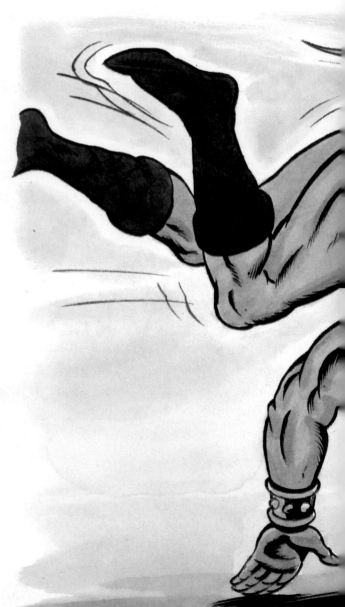

at Viper Tower and, communicating telepathically, it informed King Hiss of all that had occurred inside Man-At-Arms' laboratory.

"Ah, it seems my plan wasn't as foolproof as I imagined. I should have destroyed the weather cannon after I activated it," Hiss said to himself. "But no matter, that's an oversight that can still be rectified. This is one scheme He-Man won't foil!" He rose suddenly from his throne. "Snake Men, fetch your weapons, prepare the fighter craft — we're going to war!"

Meanwhile, inside the Pyramid of Myrabim, Man-At-Arms was sitting in the shadow of the gigantic weather cannon. He was stripped to the waist and dripping in sweat. A water bottle was held loosely in his left hand. He slowly raised it, took a sip, and sighed. Along with He-Man, he had arrived in the Desert Zone over three hours

ago, but as yet all his attempts at reversing the weather cannon's polarity had failed.

"How's the work coming along?" He-Man asked, entering the pyramid from outside.

"Slowly. Working in this heat is almost impossible, but I..."

Man-At-Arms' words were suddenly drowned out by the familiar roar of jet engines.

Racing back outside, He-Man came face to face with the Snake Men, as they leapt down from their fighter craft. "Hiss!" he yelled. "I might have known you and your cronies were behind this."

Tung Lashor darted stealthily forward, spitting his magical venom at the Eternian champion. Reacting instinctively, He-Man dived into a forward roll, athletically avoiding the sticky fluid as it spattered on the stone wall of the pyramid. He quickly leapt to his feet, but was unable to

avoid Rattlor's steel-strong tail as it was swung into his chest, propelling him backwards, into the pyramid. He was followed by the gleeful Snake Men.

"What the...?" Man-At-Arms cried, at the sudden intrusion.

"Take him," shouted King Hiss, pointing at the master scientist.

The Snake Men surged forward and surrounded Man-At-Arms. He fought bravely, but in his weakened condition he was no match for so many enemies.

"Ha! So much for Eternia's famous scientist," Sssqueeze said, wrapping his incredibly long arms around Man-At-Arms. "You're finished! Finished!"

"N-No," He-Man murmured. He had been knocked unconscious by Rattlor's blow, and was only now regaining his senses. Some distance in front of him, he could clearly see Man-At-Arms falling before the Snake Men's savage assault.

He had to save his friend, but how? Man-At-Arms was standing in front of the weather cannon. Although a well placed power-blast would certainly scatter the Snake Men, it would also destroy the ancient machine...and with it, the only chance of returning Eternia's climate to normal. Still, he couldn't leave his friend helpless...could he? For seemingly endless seconds, he struggled with this dilemma, eventually reaching a decision...

He slowly raised his Power Sword, took careful aim, and fired a blast of electricity at the band of Snake Men. It streaked towards its target, landing on the ground immediately in front of King Hiss and his followers. There was a fiery explosion that blasted the weather cannon and sent the Snake Men scurrying for safety.

"Ha, ha, ha! I don't believe it! He-Man did our job for us!" King Hiss cackled, racing out of the pyramid and back towards his fighter craft. "He did our job for us!"

Soon, the other Snake Men had joined their leader in the ship. It soared skyward, arced over the Myrabim Pyramid and disappeared from sight.

Inside the pyramid, He-Man helped Man-At-Arms to his feet. "Are you all right?" he asked.

"Y-Yes...B-But the weather cannon...Without it we're doomed!"

"Oh, I don't think so," said Orko, miraculously appearing beside Man-At-Arms. "Even though the cannon has been destroyed, I'm sure I'll be able to use my magical powers to turn the weather back to normal."

Man-At-Arms started to voice a protest, but Orko closed his eyes and began to hum softly. Magical energy danced and sparked about the little Trollan and, with obvious surprise, the Heroic Warriors began to feel it getting cooler. Eventually it was no hotter than any normal day...but still the temperature drop continued. Outside, dark clouds formed in the sky and it began to snow. Lightly at first, but then heavier.

"Orko!" Man-At-Arms cried. "You've done it again!"

"Er...well...the snow will go away," Orko said, sheepishly. "Won't it?"

But the snow didn't go away and, days later, most of Eternia was covered by a thick, white blanket.

"According to Man-At-Arms, Orko's magically induced winter will probably last for some months," Teela said, turning to Prince Adam.

The pair had returned to the Evergreen Forest and the prince was now trying to skate across the iced-over river. "Oh I don't mind," he said, "I kind of like it. Besides it's much better than that horrid summer."

"Well if you like the cold so much, you can have these!" THUMP! THUMP! Two snowballs suddenly struck Adam on his back. He tumbled and fell into a deep snowdrift that had formed on top of the frozen river.

And, back at Eternos Palace, Orko was sure he could hear the sound of Teela's distinctive, tinkling laughter.

FOR THE POWER OF GRAYSKULL

A game for two to four players.

While conducting magical experiments the Sorceress has contracted a mystical sickness, thereby leaving Grayskull open to attack. Skeletor, King Hiss and

How to play

You will need a dice and four coloured counters or buttons.

Each player chooses to be one of the four characters (He-Man, Skeletor, King Hiss or Hordak), and places their counter on the appropriate starting point. For example, on Snake Mountain if you are Skeletor.

You throw the dice to move. You must always move the number of spaces indicated on the dice, and each player must travel along their own pathway.

If you land on a yellow square, you are sucked into a Space Warp and must throw the magical number 6 to escape.